ONE FROG TOO MANY

by Mercer
and Marianna Mayer

A Puffin Pied Piper

Library of Congress Catalog Card Number: 75-6325
First Pied Piper Printing 1977
Printed in Hong Kong by South China Printing Co.
C O B E
13 15 17 19 20 18 16 14
A Pied Piper Book is a registered trademark of Dial Books for Young Readers
A member of Penguin Putnam Inc.
® TM 1,163,686 and ® TM 1,054,312
ONE FROG TOO MANY is published in a hardcover edition by
Dial Books for Young Readers, 375 Hudson Street, New York, New York 10014
ISBN 0-14-054679-0

For Phyllis Fogelman
who got the ball rolling

. . . Hats off to you